Toad Tales

Edited by
Shane Rhodes

Illustrations by Alice Beasley

Toad Tales

Edited by Shane Rhodes

ISBN 9781903110423

First published in this edition 2015 by Wrecking Ball Press.

Copyright Individual authors

Illustrations by Alice Beasley

Design by humandesign.co.uk

Introduction

When Philip Larkin used toads as a metaphor to describe his feelings about work he could not have foreseen how his poem 'Toads' would take on a life of its own. One day as if by magic there were toads everywhere in Hull. Then just as quickly as they appeared they disappeared. After what seemed like the longest hibernation they are back, living within these pages.

This book has been a labour of love for the writers, telling us stories of the toads' adventures while they were away.

You will be amazed at what they got up to!

Shane Rhodes

These tales and poems were inspired by the original Larkin with Toads designs produced by many different artists from Hull and beyond.

Toad in the Hull - Artists: Janis Goodman and Sarah Fisher

Kiss Me Quick - Artist: Stephen Mckay

Heat Toad - Artists: Alec Tear and Saul Logan

The Hidden Toad - Artist: Sasha Heath

Kasey Toad - Artists: Ian Nicholl and Emily Fisher

Twinkle Toad - Artist: Rick Welton

Space Hopper - Artists: NaSA Young People's Project and Liz Dees

Maritime Toad - Pinkyvision

Tequila Toad - Artist: Quentin Budworth

10-5 Toad - Artist: Steve Elliott

Magenta Toad - Artist: Lewis Jackson

Harlequin, Mischievous Man of Mystery - Artist: Jayne Tunnicliffe

Tiger Toad - Artist: Domanic Li

Squatwit - Artist: Ruth Pickard

Reflective Colours - Artists: Sue Kershaw and Victoria Merrett

You can see these and all the other Larkin with Toads designs at
philiplarkin.com/larkin-with-toads

Contents

A Toad In The Hull!

By Samantha Hancock

Captain Scallywag breathed in the morning air, "ARR! This be a good day for sailin'!", he exclaimed gruffly raising his telescope to his good eye, a black patch covered his other. The sun was bold and golden, high in the blue and cotton-wool clouded sky. The gigantic vessel swept through the salty sea. Master Rotter joined Captain Scallywag and took the wheel. First-Mate-Morris studied the map. Sailor Riggs climbed the riggings. Mr Swabbie mopped the decks and whistled a tune. Powder the Captains monkey nibbled a biscuit and fixed his pirate hat. This was the crew of the Roving Ruby pirate ship, the meanest, the nastiest, most filthy and foulest and fiercest pirates to roam the oceans!

All's well Captain Scallywag thought — when all of a sudden out of the kitchen ran the Cook leaving behind the hullabaloo of falling pots, pans and plates, "DOOOMED! We're all DOOOMED!!!".

"Yo-ho-ho what's got into you, you old fool?" cackled Captain Scallywag.

"Iiin tttthere..." The cook pointed to below the deck, eyes wide with fear, "Iiit's aaa GGGHOUL!!!".

Captain Scallywag, Master Rotter, First-Mate-Morris, Sailor Riggs, Mr Swabbie, and even Powder the monkey fell about laughing.

The cook, straightened himself up and held his head high to hide his embarrassment, "Go see for yourselves, you scurvy-dogs! Mark me words, I warned yee!"

So the crew, with much howling and snickering, ventured into the ships kitchen where they were greeted by a mess of saucepans and broken crockery...

...they were also greeted by the sound of a mysterious, low croaking...

... they were also greeted by the sight of a rather large imposing shadow on the furthest wall... ...they were also greeted by a pair of bulbous bulging yellow eyes hiding in the darkness... "SHIVER ME TIMBERS!!!", shrieked Captain Scallywag.

"BLIMEY!!!", screeched Master Rotter.

"Well, call me Molly and make me walk the plank..." whispered Sailor Riggs, in case the ghastly creature might hear him.

"AYE! And it's right by our best barrel of grog too!!!" worried First-Mate-Morris (who was partial to a drink or ten...more so than the rest of the crew.)

Powder the monkey squeaked and hid under Captain Scallywag's bushy beard.

"I told yers there was a GHOUL! A ghoul come to scare our souls!" the cook said in terror. "That's no ghoul – it's a MONSTER! A monster come to sink the ship!" wailed Master Rotter.

"No, it's a DEMON! A demon come to drive us mad!" cried First-Mate-Morris.

"No, it's a GREAT SEA-BEAST! A sea-beast come to gobble us up!" wailed Mr Swabbie.

The crew continued to debate who and what the mysterious creature was the only way pirates knew how – It involved a lot of shouting, and saying 'Arrrr!' and drawing of swords. "EEEEENOUGH!!!" bellowed Captain Scallywag, which was more than enough to stop the din and make everyone stand to attention.

"What be IT Cap'n? And what should we do?" shivered Master Rotter.

There was a flicker of confusion in Captain Scallywag's eye. "Cap'n, if I may?" Sailor Riggs stepped forward, "I think I know what IT be."

"Do go on me boy", said Captain Scallywag, intrigued.

Sailor Riggs carefully crept toward the ghoul-monster-demon-sea-beast, his sword in one hand, a frying pan in the other. The rest of the crew watched, jitterfied, heebie-jeebiefied. Master Rotter hid behind Captain Scallywag, First-Mate-Morris hid behind Master Rotter, Mr Swabbie hid behind First-Mate-Morris, and The Cook hid behind Mr Swabbie. Powder the monkey was still in Captain Scallywag's beard.

Just three steps left, one...two...three – Sailor Riggs raised the frying pan in the air AND - "oh!!!" breathed Sailor Riggs relieved, as he lowered the frying pan. He then proceeded to let out a hearty howl.

"Well, boy...WHAT BE IT???" growled Captain Scallywag, the crews faces poking out from behind him.

"You won't believe it, Cap'n!" Sailor Riggs yelled, tears filled his eyes from all his chuckling, "IT'S A TOAD!!!...A TOAD IN THE HULL!!!".

There was a second of silence before the whole crew fell about roaring with laughter, and the laughter did not stop for quite a while. However, when it did stop Captain Scallywag, Master Rotter, First-Mate-Morris, Sailor Riggs, Mr Swabbie, The Cook, and even Powder the monkey all agreed never to tell a living soul about the commotion the toad had caused, for after all they were the meanest, the nastiest, most filthy and foulest and fiercest pirates to roam the oceans!

Kiss Me Quick

by Karen Turner

Christopher Toad had smooth, pale skin, and large golden eyes. He lived near a garden pond, where he had tasty slugs and snails to eat, a big stone to crawl under when the sun shone too brightly, and fresh, clean water to drink.

But there was something badly wrong with Christopher Toad's life. He was all alone, and this made him sad.

"I wonder when I will meet a special someone," he said to a gentle wood mouse, who had come to the pond for a drink.

"You must find a beautiful princess, and she must kiss you," said the mouse, who had read a great number of stories. "Then you'll turn into a handsome prince, and you'll both live happily ever after."

Christopher had heard this kind of thing before, but he didn't really believe it could be true. In fact, many people had kissed him, and some of them had even left bright scarlet lipstick marks behind. His white skin was covered in red kisses, and he had never turned into a handsome prince. But then he had never been kissed by a princess.

The mouse seemed very wise, and Christopher decided to

trust his new friend.

"But how will I find a princess?" asked Christopher. "I've never seen any round here."

"You need to travel to the royal palace," said the mouse. "It's a few miles away, and I've heard that the King has three beautiful daughters. One of them is sure to be suitable."

Christopher bounced up and down on his long legs and said, "Then I must leave right away!"

He asked the mouse, "Will you come with me? You know the way, and we could keep each other company on the journey."

The mouse agreed, and they set off together through the dark night.

After many hours, as the sun was beginning to rise, Christopher and the mouse found themselves in the palace grounds, in the most splendid garden they had ever seen. There was a boating lake and a summer house. There were trees, plants and flowers of every shape and colour, all smelling so sweetly that Christopher wanted to stop and talk to them all.

But the mouse pulled him onwards, towards the open kitchen door of the palace. They could hear Cook inside, scolding the maid for burning the porridge.

Suddenly, they heard heavy footsteps marching towards them. "Come along, girls!" bawled a large woman, swinging her arms. "Daily exercises in the garden before breakfast."

Three girls came scurrying after her, blinking in the sunlight. The mouse nudged Christopher. "Those are the three princesses."

Christopher knew it was very rude to stare, but he couldn't help it. The girls were so beautiful, with rosy cheeks and twinkling eyes and smiling mouths, their hair twirling as they skipped and hopped.

He sat on the path with his mouth hanging open, and an expression of total delight and wonder on his smooth white face. One of the girls saw him and screamed. "Aagh! A horrible slimy toad!"

One of the girls saw the mouse. "Eek! A mouse!"

And they ran away into the kitchen, banging the door shut.

The third little girl gently picked Christopher up in her soft hands, and gazed into his golden eyes. "My, you're a handsome fellow," she said. She scooped up the mouse and sat him on her shoulder, saying, "Sweet, pretty mouse."

Christopher, in a nervous, croaky voice, suggested that the

princess might like to kiss him.

"Oh, silly, that's frogs, not toads," said the little princess. "Only frogs turn into handsome princes. Toads are always toads, no matter how many kisses they get. And I can see you've had a few already."

A little tear began to form in Christopher's eye, and his throat felt as if it had a snail stuck in it.

But the princess gently carried him to the side of the lake, where she turned over a flat stone. Underneath it was the most beautiful toad that Christopher had ever seen. She was green, and warty, and her eyes were very round on the top of her head. She had a wide, squatting body with broad shoulders.

When she saw Christopher, she smiled her widest ever smile and crawled towards him.

She kissed him, and they lived happily together until the end of their days. The wood mouse lived nearby and found a wife of his own, and the little princess came to play with them every day.

The Amazing Transformation Of Heat Toad

by Sam Hawcroft

Heat Toad was a lonely toad. He wasn't like all the other toads in Toadland, who were beautifully decorated in vivid colours and exciting designs. He was drab, and grey, and no-one was interested in him. All the children and their parents who came to visit Toadland would stop and have their pictures taken with every other toad but poor Heat Toad. And that made him very sad.

Heat Toad lived on his own in Larkin Street, Toad City. Every day he would hop over to the River Bank to draw out some money, before going shopping. On his way back home he would often stop by at his local pub, the Toad in the Hole, for a drink of Croaka-Cola. He would squat in a corner, alone, reading the *Toad Times*, sipping his sweet drink from a curly-wurly straw. The room would usually be full of lots of colourful toads croaking and cackling and having lots of fun. But no-one ever talked to Heat Toad.

Then he would hop all the way home, clutching his little basket of food. No-one in the street would ever stop to say hello. The tourists were too busy talking to all the other toads. It was almost as though they saw right through Heat

Toad – as though he was not even there. His grey skin just blended in to the background of plain brick buildings and wintry, rainy skies.

Heat Toad usually spent his evenings watching TV, especially during the cold, dark winter. He would never miss his favourite programme, the *Antiques Toadshow*. But sometimes he felt as though the television was his only friend.

However, one day things started to change. Spring had finally arrived – the trees started to blossom, flowers bloomed, bees buzzed, and the birds began to sing even louder. At last it started to get warmer outside. And when he went for his daily walk, Heat Toad noticed something odd. He could not be sure, but he thought that his skin did not look quite so grey. If anything, it was more light-brown. No-one else noticed, though. Still no-one stopped to say hello. He remained the most boring, dull toad in all of Toadland.

Heat Toad was back in the Toad in the Hole, ordering his Croaka-Cola, when a little boy who had come to visit Toadland with his mum and dad bumped into him, and put his hand on him to stop himself falling over. Then something amazing happened. There was now a handprint-shaped blaze of colour on Heat Toad's back. There were all the colours of the rainbow, in swirls and stripes, shining out in the dingy room as bright as the sunny day outside.

"Wow!" said the boy. "Mum! Dad! Look!" But by the time his

parents had turned around, the colour was fading, and had almost gone. But the boy was sure he'd seen it.

"Can I put my hand on your back again?" he asked Heat Toad.

Heat Toad could hardly croak an answer. This was the first time he could remember anyone speaking to him in a long time.

"W-w-w-why... y-y-y-yes... of course you can!" he managed to stutter, as the boy's parents came over to see what the fuss was about.

This time, the boy placed both hands on Heat Toad's back. Sure enough, two handprints appeared, in the most wonderful colours the boy had ever seen. His mum and dad were equally amazed, both letting out a gasp at the stunning transformation.

By now practically all the other toads and tourists had turned around to look. One by one they came up to Heat Toad and asked him politely if they could "have a go". They patted his head and his back, and shook both his hands – until almost all of his skin had turned from a dull grey-brown into a vibrant patchwork of red, yellow, green, orange, pink, blue and purple.

The little boy gave Heat Toad a great big hug, just as the colours began to fade away again. As Heat Toad's back lit up in another flash of dazzling hues, he could not help but shed a few tears. But they were tears of happiness. He really was just as fascinating as all the other toads.

And once the word had spread around Toad City, he became the most popular toad in town. People were queuing up to have their photograph taken with him, covering him with their colourful handprints. He would never be ignored again.

Hidden Toad Where Have You Been?

by Claire Bove

Croaking away your mysterious song
Hints of secrets now long gone
Of worlds unknown beneath our feet
The voices that yearn, yearn to speak

History frozen in years gone by
Beyond the tallest building's eye
To a time before the engines beeped
When a fisherman's catch was a blessed feat

Do not look at the historic gate
Unless you wish to meet their gaze
Souls that passed but still linger on
Whisper their enchanting song

Come below, come beneath
The hidden layers that no one sees
Let us whisper in your ear, the memories we hold dear
Hidden Toad sing our song, Let our memories live on!

The Toad Who Was In Fact A Toad

by Chiara Dominte

After 5 years of having been in his new town, Kiss-me-Quick was very depressed. He had earned his descriptive name by begging girls to do exactly that... and everywhere he had gone, he had been kissed till his pale white skin had reddened and he now had marks all over him where he had been unable to wipe the lipstick off.

His family had moved to Hull after he had kissed one of the princesses in London and had been kicked in return. The journey up north had been a long one and as far as Kiss-me-Quick was concerned, a useless one.

He lay at the side of the lake and pondered. It was mating season and all the other toads were busy courting and playing shy. He sighed heavily as Kasey Toad hopped by in front of him for a little longer than necessary before moving on. Kiss-me-quick just looked away. Kasey was fun, but that little sign on her side saying "proud to be part of local life" just irritated him. He deserved a real-life princess and to change into a prince. He knew he was so much better than other toads.

Once Kasey had shrugged and moved on, he hopped slowly away from the lake towards a little house that seemed to lean into the trees for support. The little girl who lived there was very polite and kind and was probably the closest thing he'd get to a princess in Hull! Jenny was a lively little girl, full of laughter and games. She had noticed Kiss-me-Quick before and spoken to him, but never kissed him.

Today however, Jenny was sitting quietly, one hand on her ball, almost perfectly still. Kiss-me-Quick hopped up close and waited. It wasn't long before she noticed him.

"Oh Toad! Why can't I be a princess? A princess is so beautiful and elegant, and I am just a small, ugly nobody!"

Kiss-me-Quick wondered whether this was a real question, and if she was talking to him. Should he answer her? He had to decide quickly, so he thought he'd give it a shot.

"I think you are beautiful, Jenny! And if you kiss me, maybe I will turn into a prince, and you can be my princess!"

Jenny laughed, and smiled at him.

"I don't think that's how it works, Toad. Not in real life. But I can kiss you anyway, if it makes you happy."

And so she did. Kiss-me-Quick sat very still as she picked him up and lifted him to her lips. The kiss was very quick, and then she lowered him back to the ground, still a toad.

"Jenny!" A voice interrupted their thoughts. It was her mother. "What are you doing, kissing that peculiar toad?"

"Oh Mummy, I want to be a princess, and he wants to be a prince, so I thought..."

Her voice trailed off as she realised how silly the whole idea had been. Jenny half-laughed and looked up at her mother.

"I guess I am meant to be me, right?"

Her mother smiled.

"Yes, Jenny. You are meant to be you. There are lots of people around here who need you more than you need to be a princess. Think of all the friends you'd leave behind, your family, the new people you meet every day... I think we all go through a stage of wanting to be a princess at some point. But then we realise that we were made to be exactly who we are!"

"Thanks, mummy... Sometimes I wish I was something more important, but I guess I do really belong here."

And off she ran.

She had left Kiss-me-Quick in a muddle. Why had she not been as disappointed as he was when he didn't turn into a prince? And what had her mother meant... He pondered hard as he hopped back to the other toads. He thought about it more that night as they all sang. And then he realised what Jenny's mother had said was true... that he wasn't meant to be anybody else. He was himself... and he was only called Kiss-me-Quick because of what he had made himself become. He smiled as he hopped lazily around the lake. This was a new day, a whole new life lay ahead of him. From now on he wanted to be called "Toad" and he'd find out what his real place in Hull was.

Twinkle Toad Goes Home

by Michelle Dee

High up a star explodes and shoots sparks across the night sky. Far below in a dusty old warehouse a big round eye opens wide and watches. The star flashes bright showering silvery light. The eye blinks, then the other. A big blue head moves. Big blue legs stretch out one by one.

Looking up, the magical star has gone and in its place millions of other little stars twinkle. Far away a church bell rings. Twinkle, fully awake now, flip-flops out of the warehouse.

In the distance Twinkle sees a road. Trucks run along it like tadpoles in a pond. Twinkle watches as the traffic whizzes by then hops out. Suddenly there's a terrible **SCREEEEEECH!** of brakes.

Twinkle jumps back and then tries again, this time making it halfway across. The trucks roar by either side. Twinkle darts out, forwards then sideways, big eyes looking left and right, then skittering forward again, Twinkle finally makes it across.

Flipping and flopping on the hard pavement Twinkle's toes become sore. Just then, Twinkle sees a fountain pool. With one leap of those big hind legs, Twinkle dives in. Splash!

Twinkle looks in the water and sees a big blue toad looking right back. The toad in the water is covered in a cloak of tiny stars. Twinkle lifts a foot. The toad in the water does the same. Twinkle blinks a big eye. The toad blinks right back. Twinkle sits at the edge of the pool and stares and feels sad. *Crrrooaaaak!* says Twinkle, but there is no answer. A heavy wet tear goes plippety-plop into the water, sending ripples across the pool, making the big blue toad disappear.

Twinkle hears the church bell ringing again, so hippety-hops alone into the night. Up ahead there is a small bridge and underneath the bridge a stream. Twinkle dives straight in, legs kicking hard and swims far from the dusty warehouse, away from the noisy road, far from the splashing fountain.

Somewhere behind a dark fin breaks the surface of the moonlit stream. A scaly body glides silently, swishing this way and that. It is the old pike that lives in the stream. The pike dislikes being disturbed by noisy blue toads. Twinkle's eyes open wide. Then, with one huge leap Twinkle is up out of the water, hopping and skipping across the lily pads.

The pike gives chase but becomes stuck, tangled up in weeds and lily fronds. Twinkle hopping so fast across the giant saucers of green, is soon far, far away downstream.

In the distance the church bells ring once more. It seems a long time since Twinkle escaped from the barn, dodged the trucks on the road and out-hopped the old pike. Now it is nearly morning.

Twinkle swims on into more water, far bigger than the fountain pool, far stronger than the stream. This water has big boats in it with lights at either end. Twinkle waves and calls out, '*Crrroaaakkk!*', but the only reply is the low Boom! as the boats pass each other.

After swimming for hours, Twinkle swims underneath a huge bridge. The bridge crosses the big river and vanishes into the mist on the far side.

Twinkle flops out of the river on to a pebbly beach to rest. Then from nowhere, '*Crrrroaaakkk!*' Twinkle looks around. Then again, '*Crrrroaakkk! Crrrroaakkk!*' Twinkle hurries towards the sound, hopping through a grass meadow and into a damp wood. There in the middle of all the trees Twinkle sees an amazing sight.

Sitting in a circle around the most inviting pond are more toads than Twinkle can count. Toads of every colour imaginable greet the morning sun with a loud *Crrroaakkk!* When they see Twinkle they fall silent and stare.

Twinkle stares back. Then, head held high, Twinkle flips and flops. Just like escaping the warehouse. Big blue head moves left and right. Just like darting between the trucks. Faster and faster Twinkle skips, just like out-hopping the old pike. Lifting up a foot, just like waving to the big boats. Twinkle Toad is dancing.

The other toads have never seen anything like it! They cheer Twinkle on to dance some more. Twinkle looks into the pond and smiles. The other toads smile right back. The toads are united and Twinkle is home. *'Crrrroaaakkk!'* exclaims Twinkle - the hoppiest, happiest toad of all.

The Space Hopper

by Tracy Liennard

Let me tell you my story. I didn't start off being a hero, at the start I was just a small green toad from the local canal collecting all the rubbish people threw in the canal. Now, I may have been small, but I had big dreams. Each night I would sit on my lily pad in the canal and croak at the moon. I looked up into the night sky and thought to myself I want to go there. Everyone on the canal laughed at me. "Who ever heard of a toad in space?" scoffed the ducks, "it's Buzz Leapfrog", laughed the water rats .

But then one day there was this competition. Space Race, the first animal to get once around the solar system and land on the moon was the winner! Now I just knew I had to enter. But with what? I didn't have a rocket. So I had to make one. I knew I couldn't do it on my own, I needed help. It took some persuading but all the animals on the canal agreed to help me.

You'd be amazed how much stuff you can find in a canal. The water rats found 5 shopping trolleys and 2 old cars. The ducks brought me a washing machine, 3 bicycles and 10 vacuum cleaners set to blow to use as my thrusters. My scrap rocket was amazing, I called it the Space Hopper. I was all ready.

Now the competition was fierce. Space Monkey was in a super rocket built by Nasa's finest brains and Rocket Dog spacecraft was amazing. Other countries had equally amazing machines and animals of all kinds were competing.

So the day of the race came. All the canal animals came to cheer me on! I must admit I was a bit nervous, my tummy felt like it was full of flies (actually it was). I put on my astrosuit, climbed into the Space Hopper and strapped myself in. We were all set to launch ... 10-9-8-7-6-5-4-3-2-1 BLAST OFF!

Off we raced, we broke speed, sound and light barriers! One by one we bounced of Mercury, and skimmed past Venus. Space Monkey was in the lead, closely followed by Rocket Dog, I was in third place. We zoomed past the moon but then the Missile Mouse got distracted and started to eat the moon (turns out it actually is made of cheese).

Cosmic Cat got tangled in the rings of Saturn, Rocket Dog was laughing so hard he crashed into Uranus. The Rocketeer Rabbit and Jetpack the Tortoise stopped to argue about who was going to win. The Super Snail ran out of fuel just as we turned the corner to zoom back to the moon. It was just me and Space Monkey left. We were neck to neck, nose to nose. Fast approaching the moon. Space Monkey edged ahead of me but then ...

My engine started to go click, click, whrrrrr, BOOM!

It exploded and catapulted me onto the moon. I landed just seconds behind Space Monkey. He was out of his rocket, racing towards the finishing line ahead of me. But then I used my secret weapon. That thing that all toads are good at … hopping! I bounced across the moon in huge graceful arcs. And with one giant leap for animal kind I landed over the finishing line just a split second before Space Monkey.

And that is how I became the most famous toad on earth. Space Monkey was a really good sport about not winning. He even gave me a lift back to earth. There were pictures of me everywhere. I had my own parade. They even named a new space centre after me. "Astrotoad the hero"! Not bad for a small green toad from the local canal.

What next? Well, I could just put my webbed feet up, but I have a taste for space now. Me and Space Monkey are planning a joint mission to see if we can find little green men on Mars.

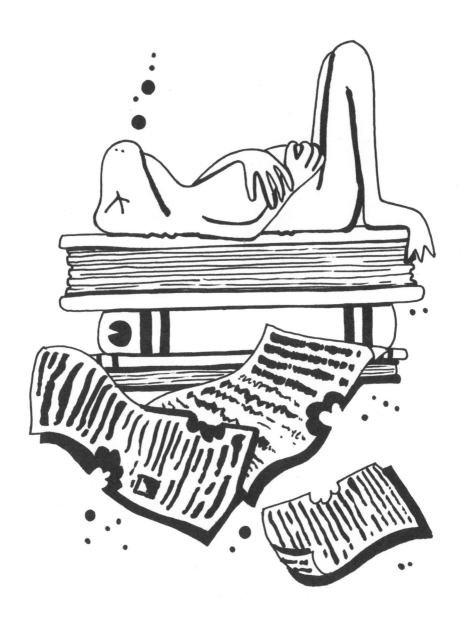

Fully Booked

by Suzanne Olivante

I have the type of face that says
I know a thing or two, or three.
Wordy-wise, a brainiac,
I feast on books of poetry
and dictionaries, story books,
growing fat and greedier,
but now I'm feeling sick...
I tried my first encyclopaedia.

Maritime Toad

by Katie Dixon

Maritime Toad lived at The Deep. It didn't have a garden but that did not matter. There were no bedrooms, but that did not matter either. Maritime Toad loved where he lived because of the water. He would watch the fish swim past all day, their scales shimmering shades of blues and greens. The seaweed would swish backwards and forwards, like it was dancing to a song. There were tiny fish, all different colours, and big fish like sharks that swam past with their sharp teeth. Maritime Toad was always friendly to them.

But one day, an idea came into Toad's head, that he would like to see a little more of the water. He wanted to swim with the fish and dance with the seaweed. He wanted to talk to the jellyfish and fall asleep happily on the sand. So one fine morning in the spring, he set off, following the long, winding road leading to the sea. The journey was more tiring than he had expected, he didn't know much about travelling. It was noisy and everything seemed ginormous. He finally reached the beach, he could hear the waves crash as they hit the sand and the seagulls were talking to each other in the sky. Toad jumped over the seaweed. It wasn't dancing this time. It was cold and slippery and crackled under his webbed feet. But he was here at last! He jumped into the sea, and swam with all his might. He kicked his legs out and pushed against the current of the ocean. It was more gray and far more cold than he was expecting. After many minutes of swimming, he looked back at the beach he had been standing on. It was tiny now. He put his head under the water and swam deeper down. He saw fish of all different colours as they dotted around the rocks. Suddenly the tail of a beautiful fish caught his eye. It was purple and shimmered as the sunlight from above the ocean hit its scales. He had begun to swim towards it when he noticed a long lock of blonde hair was floating in the water.

'Hello! Can you help me?' it said, suddenly. It was a mermaid. Toad had only ever heard of mermaids before. This one was a lot bigger than Toad, but she seemed friendly. He wondered what she wanted. 'I seem to have lost my crown. It has green flowers in it, would you help me look for it?' she asked. Toad smiled and nodded. 'Thank you! I think it fell off while I was swimming, we should try and look down there,' she said, pointing to the sand below. Toad searched high and low, behind every little rock on the floor. He searched for so long that it soon grew dark and the moonlight cast his shadow on the floor. It was no use, the crown was lost. But then, Toad noticed a shell on the ground and inside it were some shiny, white pearls. This gave Toad an idea.

The mermaid swam up to him, 'Did you find my crown?' she asked. Toad shook his head, the mermaid was disappointed until Toad held out the pearls, which he had threaded on a thin piece of weed. 'What a beautiful necklace!' the mermaid said. Toad handed her it gently. She tied it around her neck, and the pearls sparkled. They suited her perfectly! The mermaid took Toad to her home and they entered a room which was filled with people. Toad had never seen so much food on one table before. There was scrambled fish eggs, seaweed salad, salted caramel fudge and many other things. That night, he ate as much food as he could fit in his belly, he talked to the jellyfish and danced with the porpoises for hours.

He liked the sea. It did not have a garden but that did not matter, there were no bedrooms, but that did not matter either. Maritime Toad loved the sea because of his new friends and that night after the mountain of food and hours of dancing, he fell asleep happily on the soft bed of sand.

Tequila Toad And The Heat

Written at an Artlink workshop by children and
volunteers of the Mitchell Community Centre
After School Activity Session

Tequila Toad lived in a hot land. So hot that the sun shone
bright and strong all day, and there was very little shade.

If Tequila Toad didn't get in the shade he would get hot and
sweaty and bad-tempered, so he was always looking for shady
places to sit.

He found a favourite shady place and went there often, but
one day he hopped over to his special shady place and Heat
Toad was sitting there. Heat Toad glowed hot all the time, and
he also liked to be in the shade, otherwise his skin would burn.

Tequila Toad tried to hop away but Heat Toad followed him.

'Let's be friends,' croaked Heat Toad.

'No!' said Tequila Toad. He could feel himself getting hotter
and angrier with the sunshine and the heat from Heat Toad.

'Please, I haven't got any friends,' croaked Heat Toad sadly,
'everyone I know loves the sunshine, and you and I need the
shade. We could be great friends, sitting in the shade together.'

They decided to get together and come up with a plan to cope with their burning issues. Tequila Toad was getting hot and Heat Toad was getting hotter.

Both toads needed to let off steam to become cooler, so they decided to look for Twinkle Toad to make the cool night time come quicker.

'Please help us,' croaked Tequila Toad and Heat Toad, when they found Twinkle Toad, 'we can't cope with the heat, and we want to be friends and we want to be happy. Bring the cool night, because we've run out of shade.'

Twinkle Toad flung his cloak of stars across them all, protecting them from the blazing sunshine.

'This is lovely,' they all croaked.

The three toads spent their days sitting happily in the starry night shade of Twinkle Toad's cloak, having picnics on the hill, croaking contentedly, and became great friends.

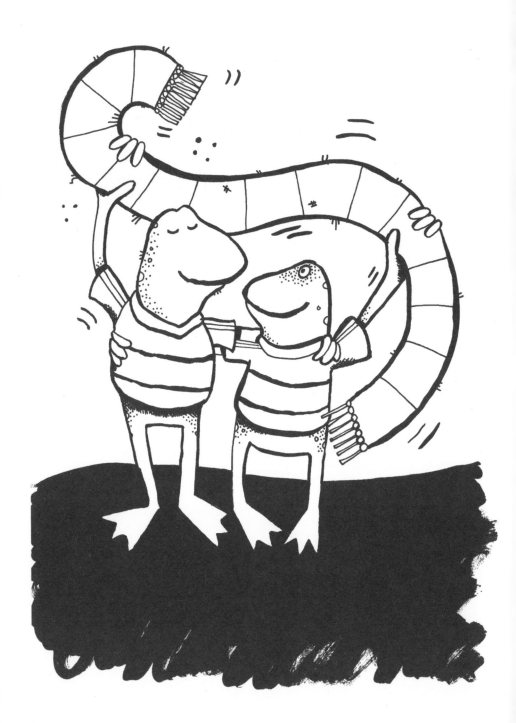

10-5 Toad

by Nick Quantrill

The rugby ball flew through the air, my eyes widening as it came hurtling down from the sky towards me. I didn't move out of the way quickly enough. The ball bounced up off the turf at Craven Park, my favourite place in the whole world, and hit me square on the nose, knocking me off my webbed feet and sending me crashing backwards into a world of darkness.

I don't know what happened, but when I opened my eyes, I wasn't at Craven Park. I didn't recognise where I was. I was sat at the side of another rugby pitch. It was loud, too loud for a toad, and colourful. I looked to my left and saw black and white flags being waved by thousands of people. I recognised the song they were singing ....*Old Faithful*... and I didn't like it. I turned to my right and looked at the sea of red and white flags. I also recognised the song they were singing ...*Red Red Robin*... and I liked it a lot more.

The people I could see in front of me looked funny, like they were from a different time. Their clothes were old-fashioned and no one was holding up a mobile phone to take a selfie. When the two sides walked out of the tunnel and lined up to play, I knew where I was. It made sense. I was at Wembley Stadium in London and the year was 1980. I was at the side of the pitch, right on the half-way line, the best view in the house. I was going to watch The Challenge Cup Final and the biggest ever Hull derby.

I felt someone tap me on the shoulder and nearly jumped out of my toad skin when I realised it was my grandad. A big grin broke out on my face as I waved my red and white scarf in the air. We both cheered as the Hull KR team kicked the match off.

Derby matches are special, Grandad Toad told me. It was east against west, the city split down the middle by its muddy river. Most of the crowd was from Hull, that much was obvious. Grandad Toad told me someone had left a big sign attached to the Humber Bridge, asking the last person to leave to turn the lights off.

We both shuffled a little closer to the touchline, watching the match. I was wearing the same shirt as the Rovers' players on the pitch. It was white with a big red band across the middle, three red stripes down each sleeve and a red collar. It felt amazing. I didn't care so much for the black and white pattern of the Hull FC shirt.

We both cheered as Rovers raced into a quick lead. Grandad Toad jumped for joy as his favourite player, Steve Hubbard, scored the first try of the match. The black and white half of the stadium was very quiet indeed. I couldn't stay still as Rovers kept up the pressure, forcing them further and further back. It was so exciting, I was sure Grandad Toad shouted out a few words my mother and father had told me to never use.

The game went on. We cheered wildly as Steve Hubbard kept on scoring points. I couldn't say the same for the kicker on the other team. There wasn't long left and Grandad Toad hugged me tightly, unable to watch the last few minutes, the score 10-5 to our beloved Rovers. The game ended, our heroes falling to the floor, exhausted. I looked across to where the red and white flags were flying high with pride, Hull KR kings of the world for a day.

Grandad Toad shouted at me to duck, the match ball kicked high into the air by one of the losing players. I watched as it started to fall out of the sky, heading straight for me. I turned to look at Grandad Toad, but he was hopping around celebrating and joining in with the supporters' songs, having the time of his life. I smiled as the ball came closer and closer to me, about to hit me square on the nose. I was ready to go back.

Tarquin The Tap Dancing Toad

(inspired by Twinkle Toad and Magenta Toad)

by Julie Anna Douglas

Tarquin Twinkle Toad spends his days,
relaxing by the lake,
but when the stars come out, he transforms,
with a shimmy and a shake.
He puts on his best bow-tie,
and perfect, tall top-hat
and skips off down the garden path,
with a rat-a-tat-tat-tat.
He tap dances round the fountain,
and spins up and down the street,
dazzling all the passers-by
with his fantastic, fancy feet.
He splish-splashes through the puddles
and with a gentle, swooshing glide
reaches the pond in the park,
and gazes with love and pride,
as the marvellous Magenta
floats softly into sight,
and the two toads twirl together
under the silvery moonlight.

Harlequin Saves The Day

by Terry Luty

Harlequin was different to all the other toads. But there was nothing wrong with that. His mum had told him on the very first day he hopped into the world "Different is good, who wants to be the same as everyone else?" Harlequin had lots, and I really do mean lots, of brothers and sisters. In fact, there were so many of them that some had to leave the pond and go out into the big city, just to have room to hop around without accidentally standing on each other. Harlequin went off with his brother, Weather Rain or Shine to live in Queen's Gardens. Although it was a really nice place to live, with lots of people and other toads to talk to, was not what Harlequin saw as his destiny. He dreamt of a place where he could be a star, a famous toad that future generations of toads would look back on fondly and say to each other, "Remember Harlequin? What a great toad he was!"

One day, when no one was around, Harlequin told his brother that it was time for him to go out into the big world outside Hull, and seek his fortune. He wrote a note for his mum and family, telling them not to worry, that he loved them all and would come back one day soon, when he was a famous toad. Then, with a final look around the garden, he hopped down the road to the station, and climbed aboard the first train he came to. He had absolutely no idea where he was going, but was pretty sure it was going somewhere nice, as all the people were smiling, and the smaller ones were carrying brightly coloured plastic buckets and spades, whilst the bigger ones had picnic baskets and rugs. Harlequin had no idea where they were going, but he couldn't wait to get there!

Once the train left the city, it quickly sped through villages and green fields, stopping every now and then to let more passengers on and off. Harlequin sat looking out of the window, fascinated by the new and wonderful things he saw. It wasn't long before the train arrived at the last stop, all the people got off, laughing and joking, carrying their buckets and spades. Harlequin hopped down from the train and followed them.

He walked down the street, taking in everything. There were guesthouses and hotels, amusements and café's selling ice creams and doughnuts and shops selling the brightly coloured buckets and spades. Beyond this, Harlequin could see the largest pond that any toad in toad history had ever seen. It seemed to go on forever! He asked one of the small people who were walking along with him "Where are we?" "At the seaside of course" said the small person. "Oh, of course, what a silly toad I am, and what's that big pond?" The little person giggled. "That's the sea".

Harlequin walked towards the pond, or the sea as the little person had told him it was called. Just before he reached it, his eyes were drawn to a small group of people, they were dressed like him! They had the same red, blue and yellow diamonds, and the same masks as him! He hopped over to them as fast as he could hop. "Hello, I'm Harlequin." The people greeted him with very sad faces. "Why are you sad?" he asked. "We are all clowns. We entertain the people on the beach with our juggling and acrobatics, but our friend is ill, so we can't put on our show today and all these people have come to see us" replied one of the clowns. "Can I help?" he asked them. "Can you jump and flip, and do somersaults?" Harlequin smiled." Of course, after all hopping, jumping and flipping is what toads do best!" "Ok" said the clown, "we have our show!".

The show was a big success, Harlequin jumped and flipped like he had never done before. The people cheered and clapped and even the clowns said it was their best ever show, with Harlequin as the star. When the time came for them to pack up, the clowns all begged him to stay for the rest of summer, but even though he had enjoyed being with them, Harlequin couldn't wait to get on the train to Hull, back to his family to tell them all about how he had been a star for a day!

The Terrifying Travels Of Tiger The Toad

by Deanna Houghton

Tiger the toad, unlike most of his kind, hated the rain. The wet sloppy drops of ice cold water, sliding down his skin like slime. Instead, he liked the sun, the bright golden rays of warm light that made his skin look shiny.

It was for this reason, that Tiger hopped unhappily through the puddles on the pavement, roaring angrily as water splashed him in the face. When he roared, he showed everyone his sharp white teeth, causing all the other toads nearby to scurry away in fear. They had been playing joyfully, jumping in and out of the small pools of rain water like schoolchildren beside him. Now, they were gone far away from the streets of Hull, back into the shadows of the local parks and ponds.

Tiger enjoyed being on his own, far away from the stares and whispers of the other toads. He didn't have their green colouring, or their beady black little eyes. Instead, he had orange and black striped skin and hypnotising brown eyes. They were afraid of him because of this, of his beauty and his ferocity. Tiger hated how they left him out of everything. They wouldn't play hopscotch with him, or noughts and crosses. He wanted friends who'd accept him, who wouldn't look at him and see him as not the same and scary. He wanted someone he could play hide and seek with, who wouldn't run away, pretend to hide and never come back. Tiger hated admitting this to himself, but despite liking his own company, he was lonely, as lonely as could be.

It was then that Tiger had an interesting thought. Perhaps he could go and find the other toads and apologise for scaring them away. Maybe if he was kind to them, he could show them that he could be their friend, that he wasn't very different compared to them, not really. They would catch flies together and race each other for fun. He smiled as he had these thoughts, hopping happily away into Pearson Park.

He was so distracted by his new found plans, that he didn't notice anything at first. He was whistling and leaping across the earth as if all were normal. It was only when he heard a loud roar, louder even than any he could make, that he realised. This wasn't Pearson Park after all. He looked up, eyes widening and blinked, as if expecting the image before him to waft away like smoke.

He was in some sort of jungle. There were birds of bright colours, red and blue and yellow flying through the sky. Birds he had never ever seen before in his entire life. There were strange purple plants also and trees so tall, that he could not stretch his neck back far enough to see the tops of them. There were other animals too, strange creatures with thick orange fur and long limbs swinging from tree to tree.

Suddenly, he heard something moving behind him. The pad of a paw tapping the earth lightly, a light growl. He turned around, slowly. There, before him stood that which he had never seen before. Something that looked... rather like him.

A Tiger. Not a toad Tiger, but a real one, with long sharp white claws and teeth. Its thick orange and black fur hanging from its body messily, tossed this way and that by the wind as it had run. It looked beautiful, more so than Tiger, even in its ferocity. It blinked slowly, turning is head to the side curiously, all signs of its previous predatory nature... gone. It didn't attack, but waited for Tiger the toad to come forward, patiently.

Tiger was scared, shaking a little having seen the size of the creature before him, but he wanted to be strong, courageous and so he stood his ground. Then, slowly and cautiously, he began to step forward, until he was only standing but a step away from the real tiger before him.

They spoke to each other then, introducing themselves. Eventually, they became friends and spent time with each other, helped each other, trusted each other with their deepest secrets. The other toads, the green ones, had ended up in the same place as Tiger also. Tiger spoke to them and this time they listened and didn't laugh at him, instead over time they accepted him as their friend too. Tiger was never lonely again.

The Voyage Of Squatwit

by Jane Ellis

Squatwit Toad dwelt near the pier,
For several weeks he settled here
As many people, large and small,
Young and old, all came to call.

Although he knew he wouldn't be
Here for years for folks to see,
Unlike the golden king and horse
And William Wilberforce of course,
He was content to stay awhile
And make the passing people smile.
As he watched the world go by
Beneath both cloud and sunny sky
He planned what he was going to do
When his time in Hull was through.

Squatwit Toad dwelt near the pier
And yearned for his own ship to steer
And dreamt one day he'd sail away
Where tides and stars and waves held sway.

At first he couldn't see a way,
He thought he'd have to stow away,
Find a ship at anchor moored
And try to creep unseen aboard
But oh, if then he should be caught
All his dreams would come to nought,
He would be returned to shore,
A landlocked toad for evermore
Who'd never sail on waters deep
Or feel the waves rock him to sleep.

Squatwit Toad dwelt near the pier
And held his hopes and wishes near
And hoped that he would have a chance
To join the tide's unending dance.

Then one day an idea struck
That, maybe, with a bit of luck,
Although it seemed a chance remote,
Maybe Squatwit Toad would float!
And so one night he boldly leapt,
While all around the city slept,
And landed with an icy shiver
In the slowly flowing river.
He sank, he rose, he turned, he spun.
Squatwit's journey had begun.

Squatwit Toad dwelt near the pier
Until his future became clear.
The river bore the toad along
On currents steady, firm and strong.

The first sights that Squatwit saw
The stars above, the lights on shore
As he set off upon his trip
Without the need to board a ship.
From river to the open sea
Our toad is happy, roaming free.
Tankers, ferries, fishing boats,
The foghorn's boom, the driftwood floats,
Among them Squatwit bobs along
Accompanied by the seabirds' song.

Squatwit Toad dwelt near the pier.
The memory of it he holds dear
But it was time to sail away
And he's still sailing to this day.

The Toad Who Wanted To Be A Prince

by Catherine Goble

Have you ever been told if you kiss a toad he will turn into a handsome prince? My Mummy and Daddy used to tell me that story when I was just a little tadpole.

From that moment, I knew I wanted to be a handsome prince one day. So, five years ago, when I was finally old enough to go out and explore on my own, I decided to find as many animals as possible to give me a kiss.

As I set off on my travels, Mummy and Daddy kissed me goodbye – but that didn't work. I was still a toad.

I went to the next door pond to see my Granny and she gave me a big, sloppy kiss. Why do Grannies always do that?! But that didn't work either. It was just wet and slimy. A bit like me.

So, I thought, where is a good place to go in Hull to meet lots of animals? Of course, East Park! They have a zoo there, and a big pond, there must be several animals there who wouldn't mind giving me a kiss. Especially if I turned into a handsome prince! Maybe I could invite them round to my palace for tea. After all, if I was a prince, I would have to live in a palace.

I liked this plan.

I hopped along to East Park and the first animal I met was a goat. He gave me a kiss, but his beard was all scratchy. I didn't like that much. So, I tried a woolly sheep. Her fleece was all soft. I enjoyed cuddling her. But I was still a toad.

All the other animals had wandered over to see what was happening. I explained that a toad could turn into a handsome prince when it was kissed. Everyone wanted to try! I had never been so popular.

They all lined up – rheas, alpacas, wallabies, ducks, and even deer. One by one they puckered up their lips and planted a kiss on my nose. Even the guinea pigs had a go at kissing me, but they could only reach my webbed feet.

But still nothing. I thanked them all for trying and went on my way. I wasn't going to give up. You should never give up on reaching your dreams, however difficult they may seem. Have your Mummy and Daddy told you that too? Mummies and Daddies are very clever.

Where next? I know – The Deep! I always feel at home there. It must be all the water. Maybe the penguins would give me a kiss? They always look so smart in their black and white outfits; I would definitely fit in with them when I turned into a handsome prince. So, off I hopped.

I had to sneak past the staff. I didn't want them to think I had escaped from one of the tanks and try to put me back. I would never become a handsome prince if I was stuck in a tank. And I would never see my Mummy and Daddy again. Or Granny. But at least that would mean no more sloppy kisses!

I hid until the coast was clear and then launched myself into the penguin area. They were very surprised to see a toad on the ice. They stopped swimming and came over to give me a kiss. I shut my eyes and wished, as their beaks pecked me on the cheek. But still nothing happened.

So, feeling sad, I hopped back into the city centre and sat down next to the statue in Queen Victoria Square. A little girl came running over, pointing and shouting to her Mummy and Daddy. She picked me up in her tiny hands. She looked at me and smiled, and bent her face towards mine. "STOP!" her parents shouted. "You don't know where he's been!"

But it was too late. She had kissed me! And, right in front of their eyes, my webbed feet grew toes and fingers, I stood on two legs, and I had hair and a golden crown on my head.

It worked! The little girl's kiss had turned me into a real little boy. I hadn't given up, and now I was a handsome prince at last.

I was so happy. The little girl was happy. Even her Mummy and Daddy were happy. And I told them exactly where I had been – on lots of exciting adventures around Hull!

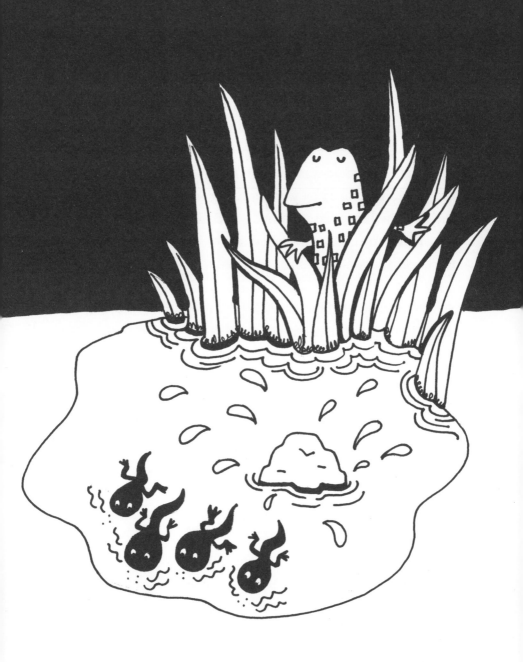

The Magic Wishing Toad

by Amy O'Sullivan

Rufus sat very still at the bottom of the pond. He knew that if he squeezed his eyes tightly shut nobody could see him. His beautiful colours blended in perfectly with the mosaic tiles in the pond so it was a good hiding place.

You might be wondering why a splendid toad like Rufus would want to hide. Well, Rufus was no ordinary toad. In fact he was a magic toad, with the power to grant wishes. The problem was that word of these powers had spread and now it seemed that everybody in the town wanted to find the toad and have a wish granted by him. Rufus didn't mind granting wishes to nice people, but unfortunately not everyone was nice.

Splash!

A large stone crashed through the water narrowly missing the toad.

Oh no, thought Rufus, not Simon again. Simon was a spoilt, selfish boy who lived in the town. He came to the pond every day to look for the toad, and each day he had a new wish to add to his long list.

"Where are you magic toad?" Simon sang, picking up another stone to throw.

Rufus tried hard to keep perfectly still as the stone landed close to his foot.

Simon kicked at the rocks surrounding the pond.

"Where are you?" he asked again. "I want you to grant me a wish!"

He kicked at the rocks again, causing one to fall into the pond, scaring the little tadpoles who swam there.

"Stupid toad!" said Simon angrily, "I bet you don't even exist!"

He bent down to pick up a large, sharp rock.

"Don't!"

A small boy stepped out from behind the hedge where he had been watching.

Simon sighed.

"Go away Rory."

"Stop throwing stones!" Rory said.

"I need to find this magic toad", said Simon. "I want a new bike!"

"Well he's not going to grant your wish if you throw stones at him" Rory said.

"He doesn't exist anyway!" Simon said "You're stupid if you believe in him". He threw the rock on the floor and pedalled away on his bike.

Rory went over to the pond and peered in.

"I'm sorry about that", he said, sitting down on the grass. "I'm sure you do exist".

Rufus opened one eye.

"He doesn't need a new bike anyway", said Rory. "He already has a very nice bike. I wish I had a bike like that." He looked sad.

Rufus swam up to the top of the pond, and climbed onto a lily pad.

Rory gave a little gasp of surprise.

"I knew you existed" he said shyly.

"Of course I exist" said Rufus "I just choose not to show myself to people like Simon. Now, would you like a bike?"

"Pardon?" Rory wasn't sure that he had heard correctly.

"I grant wishes, remember?" said Rufus "You said you wished you had a bike like his."

"Oh", said Rory, "Actually there is something I would rather wish for".

"Oh yes?" said Rufus.

"My mum isn't very well", said Rory sadly. "What I would really wish for is for her to get better again".

Rufus smiled. "That's a very nice wish" he said "Consider it done". He dived back under the water.

"Thank you!" said Rory and ran home to see his mother.

"Mum!" He called out as he went through the door.

His mother was in the garden. It was the first time she had been up and about for weeks.

"It's strange but I suddenly feel so much better" she said to him.

Rory smiled to himself but didn't tell her that he the reason why.

"Look Rory, another strange thing has happened." she said, pointing behind her. "This just appeared out of nowhere".

It was a shiny new bike, much nicer than Simon's!

Rory ran over to look at it.

"It has such an unusual pattern" his mother said "like a mosaic."

Rory grinned, thinking about exactly where he had seen that pattern before.

"Thank you, magic toad!" he thought as he hopped onto the bike.

Toad Tales was created as part of the Toads Revisited programme, celebrating 5 years since the Larkin25 commemoration of the life and work of the poet, novelist, librarian and jazz critic, Philip Larkin, and also marking the 30th Anniversary of his death. We would like to thank our funders and sponsors for their support.

Supported by Hull UK City of Culture 2017